The Little Mermaid

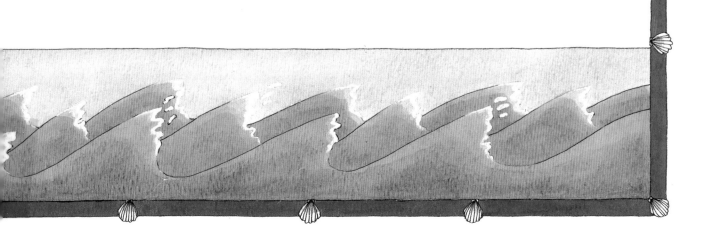

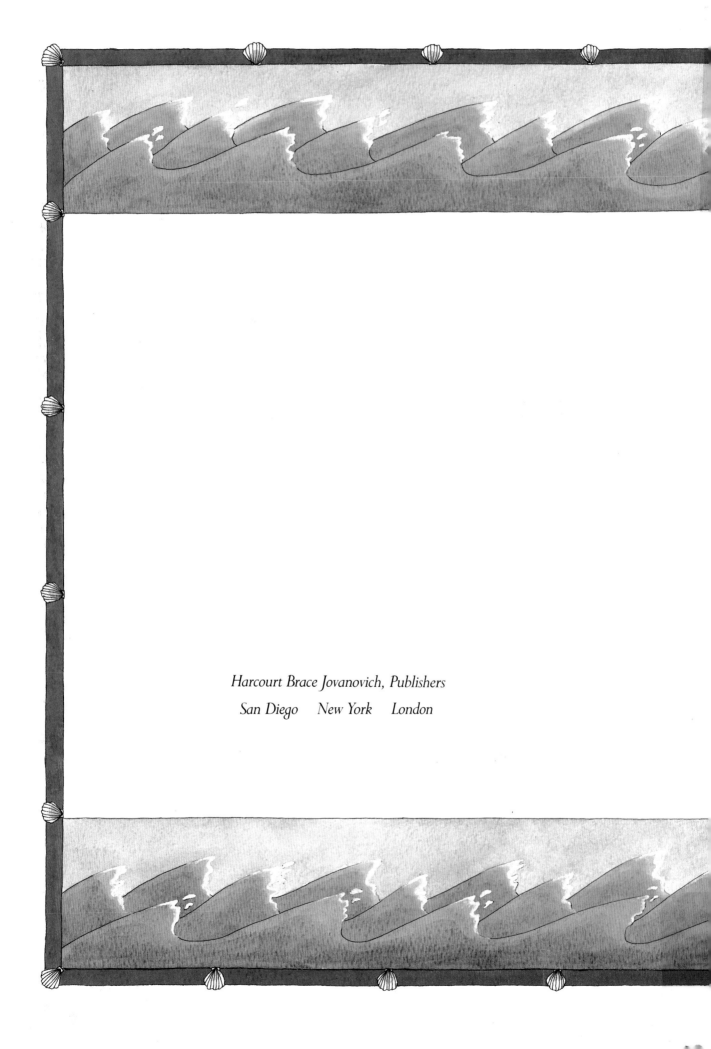

Harcourt Brace Jovanovich, Publishers

San Diego   New York   London

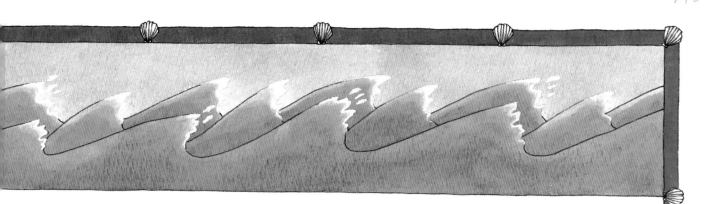

HANS CHRISTIAN ANDERSEN
The Little Mermaid

Illustrated by

KATIE THAMER TREHERNE

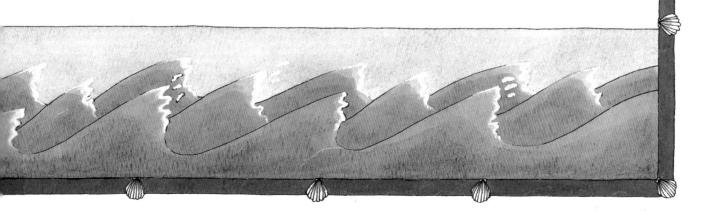

For Thomas Michael Justin
—K. T. T.

This text for The Little Mermaid was adapted by the editors
from the 1942 edition of Andersen's Fairy Tales, translated
from the Danish by Jean Hersholt, published by The Heritage
Press, and used by permission.

Library of Congress Cataloging-in-Publication Data
Treherne, Katie Thamer.
The little mermaid / Hans Christian Andersen;
illustrated by Katie Thamer Treherne. — 1st ed.
p.   cm.
Summary: A little mermaid sacrifices her lovely voice
and her fishtail in order to become human and
have a chance to marry the prince she loves
and earn an immortal soul.
ISBN 0-15-246320-8
[1. Fairy tales. 2. Mermaids—Fiction.]   I. Andersen, H. C.
(Hans Christian), 1805–1875. Lille havfrue. English. II. Title.
PZ8.T7641i   1989
[Fic]—dc19   89-31602

First edition   A B C D E

HBJ

A Note about the Author

Hans Christian Andersen was born in 1805 in Odense, the second-largest city in the small country of Denmark. His family was poor — his mother a washerwoman, his father a cobbler — but throughout his childhood Andersen's father read him tales from *The Arabian Nights* and even built him a toy theater. On that stage, young Andersen lived in the plays of Shakespeare and with characters of his own devising. He learned to sing, dance, and recite and often performed in the local theater.

At the age of fourteen, taking all of his savings, Andersen set out for the sparkling capitol city of Copenhagen, where he hoped to make his way in the theater. With help from friends, he was admitted to schools and was given small parts in theatrical performances. But his first major audition was a humiliating experience, and the plays he wrote were all rejected.

Then in 1835, the year he published his first book of stories, *Tales Told for Children*, Andersen's fortunes changed dramatically. His reputation as a storyteller spread quickly around the world, and he traveled widely, visiting the brothers Grimm in Germany and Charles Dickens in England.

Yet throughout his life the deep pain and insecurity of his early years remained with Andersen. Although he was able to transform that pain into beautiful, sometimes humorous tales, the story of the sensitive and virtuous soul who goes unrecognized and suffers in silence is one that Andersen repeats again and again, as in this story of *The Little Mermaid* who comes to the city full of hope when she is fifteen — a year older than Andersen was when he first came to Copenhagen — and sacrifices her lovely voice for a chance to marry the prince she loves.

— PETER F. NEUMEYER

Professor, English and Comparative Literature
San Diego State University

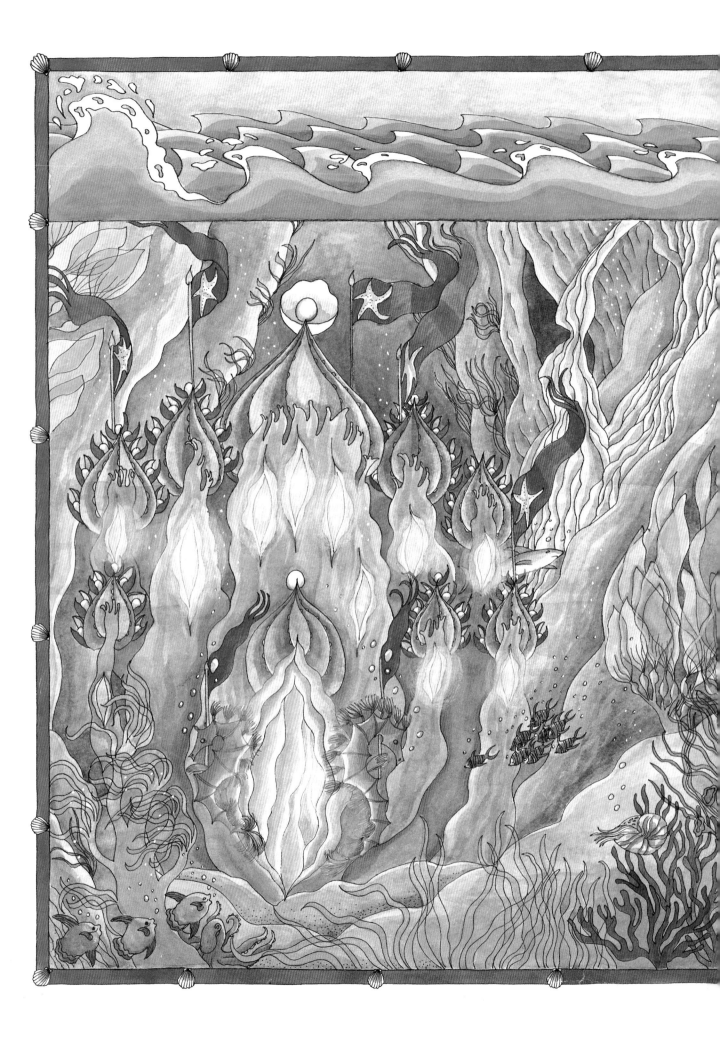

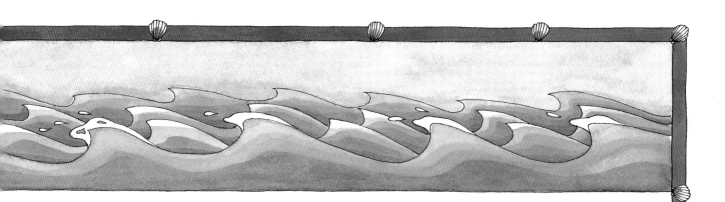

*F*ar out in the ocean the water is as blue as the petals of the loveliest cornflower and as clear as the purest glass. It goes deeper than any anchor rope will go, and it is down there that the sea folk live.

Now don't suppose that there are only bare white sands at the bottom of the sea. No, indeed! The most marvelous trees and flowers grow there. All sorts of fish, large and small, dart among the branches, just as birds flit through the trees up here. From the deepest spot in the ocean rises the palace of the sea king. Its walls are made of coral and its high pointed windows are of the clearest amber, but the roof is made of mussel shells that open and shut with the tide. Every shell holds glistening pearls, any one of which would be the pride of a queen's crown.

The sea king had been a widower for years, and his old mother kept house for him. She was extremely fond of her granddaughters, the six little sea princesses. They were all lovely, but the youngest was the most beautiful. Her skin was as soft and tender as a rose petal, and her eyes were as blue as the deep sea, but like her sisters, her body ended in a fishtail.

Outside the palace was a big garden, with flaming red and deep blue trees. Each little princess had her own small plot, where she could dig and plant whatever she liked. One of them made her little flower bed in the shape of a whale, another shaped hers like a little mermaid, but the youngest made hers as round as the sun. She was an unusual child, quiet and wistful, and she would allow nothing in her garden except flowers as red as the sun and a marble statue of a handsome boy that she had found in a sunken ship. Beside the statue she planted a rose-colored weeping willow tree.

Nothing gave the youngest princess such pleasure as to hear about the world of human beings up above them. She made her old grandmother tell her all she knew about ships and cities, people and animals.

"When you get to be fifteen," her grandmother said, "you will be allowed to rise up out of the ocean and sit on the rocks in the moonlight, to watch the great ships sailing by. You will see woods and towns, too."

Next year the eldest princess had her fifteenth birthday and received permission to rise up out of the water. When she got back she had a hundred things to tell her sisters, but the most marvelous thing of all, she said, was to lie on a sandbar in the moonlight, gazing at the large city on the shore, where the lights twinkled like hundreds of stars, to listen to music, to hear the clatter and clamor of carriages and people.

Oh, how intently the youngest sister listened. After this, whenever she sat at her open window at night and looked up through the dark blue waters, she thought of that great city with all of its clatter and clamor.

The next year, her second sister had permission to rise to the surface and swim wherever she pleased. She went up just at sunset, and she found that spectacle the most marvelous she had ever seen. The heavens had a golden glow, and a flock of wild swans flew toward the setting sun.

The following year, her third sister ascended, and, as she was the boldest of them all, she swam up a broad river that flowed into the ocean. In a small cove, mortal children were paddling about in the water. She wanted to play with them, but they took fright and ran away. Then along came a little black animal — it was a dog, but she had never seen a dog before. It barked at her so ferociously she took fright herself and fled to the open sea.

The fourth sister was not so venturesome. She stayed far out among the rough waves, which she said was a marvelous place. She saw ships, but they were so far away they looked like sea gulls.

Now the fifth sister had her turn. Her birthday came in the wintertime, so she saw things that none of the others had seen. The sea was a deep green color, and enormous icebergs drifted about. They assumed the most fantastic shapes and glistened like pearls.

On many an evening the older sisters would rise to the surface, arm in arm, all five in a row. They had beautiful voices, more charming than those of any human beings. When a storm was brewing and they anticipated a shipwreck, they would swim before the ship and sing, trying to overcome the sailors' fear of the bottom of the ocean. But people could not understand their song and mistook it for the voice of the storm.

Their youngest sister stayed behind all alone, wanting to weep. But a mermaid has no tears, and therefore she suffers much more than humans.

"Oh, how I do wish I were fifteen!" she said. "I know I shall love that world up there and all the people who live in it."

Then at last she, too, came to be fifteen.

"Come, let me adorn you like your sisters," said her grandmother. In the little mermaid's hair she put a wreath of white lilies made of pearls. And the old queen fastened oysters to the princess's tail, as a sign of her high rank.

The red flowers in her garden were much more becoming to the little mermaid, but she didn't dare to make any changes. "Good-bye," she said, and up she went through the water, as light and sparkling as a bubble.

The sun had just gone down when her head rose above the surface, but the clouds still shone like gold and roses and the evening star gleamed in the sky. The air was mild and fresh and the sea unruffled. A great three-master lay in view with only one of its sails set, for there was not even the whisper of a breeze. Music and singing rang from the ship, and as night came on the sailors lighted hundreds of brightly colored lanterns.

The little mermaid swam right up to the window of the main cabin and peered in through the clear glass panes at the crowd of people within. She saw a young prince with big dark eyes, who could not have been more than sixteen years old. It was his birthday, and that was the reason for the celebration. Oh, how handsome the prince was! He laughed and he smiled and shook hands with people while the music rang out in the perfect evening.

It grew very late, but the little mermaid could not take her eyes off the ship and the prince. The brightly colored lanterns were blown out, and the ship began to sail.

Then there was a rumble deep down in the sea, great clouds gathered, and lightning flashed in the distance. Ah, they were in for a terrible storm. Waves rose up like towering black mountains, and the tall ship pitched and rolled. To the little mermaid this seemed good sport, but not to the sailors. The ship creaked, thick timbers gave way, the mainmast snapped in two, and water burst into the hold.

One moment it would be black as pitch, and the little mermaid couldn't see a thing. Next moment the lightning flashed so brightly that she could see every person on board. She watched closely for the prince, and when the ship split in two, she saw him sink down in the sea. At first she was overjoyed that he would be with her, but then she recalled that humans could not live under water. No, he must not die! So she swam among the floating planks and beams, forgetting they might crush her. She dived through the waves until she reached the prince, and held his head above the water.

At daybreak, when the storm was over, not a trace of the ship was in view. The mermaid kissed the prince's forehead, but his eyes remained closed. As she stroked his wet hair, it seemed to her that he looked like the marble statue in her garden. She kissed him again and hoped that he would live.

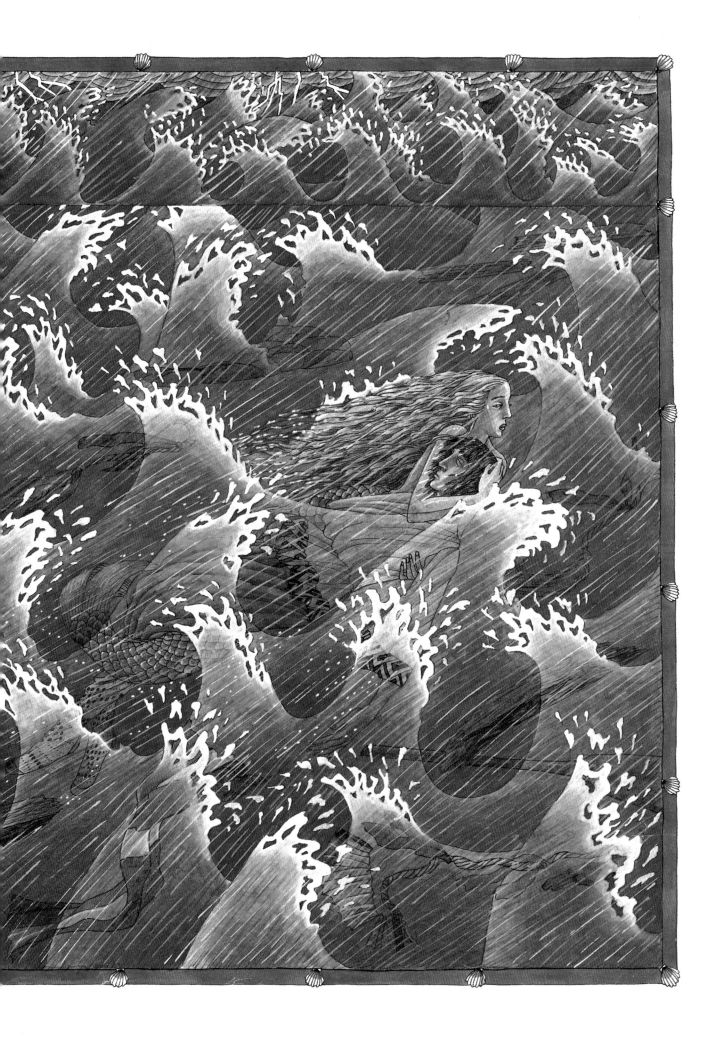

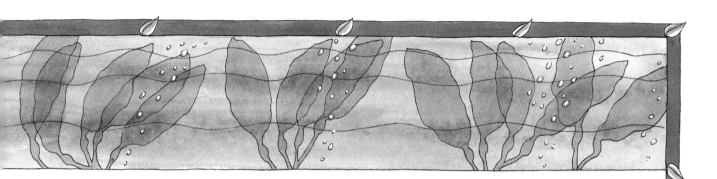

Soon she saw dry land rise before her. Fine white sand had washed up below the cliffs. She swam there with the prince and stretched him out on the sand, taking special care to pillow his head up high in the warm sunlight.

Bells began to ring in a great white building near the beach, and a number of young girls came outside. The little mermaid swam away behind some tall rocks, and then she watched to see who would find the poor prince.

Soon one of the girls came upon him. The little mermaid watched the prince regain consciousness and smile at those who had gathered around. But he did not smile at her, for he did not even know she had saved him. Sadly she dived down into the water and returned to her father's palace. Her sisters asked her what she had seen on her first visit up to the surface, but she would not tell them a thing.

Many evenings and many mornings she revisited the spot where she had left the prince, but she never saw him and came home each time sadder than when she had left. She would sit in her garden with her arms about the beautiful marble statue that resembled the prince. But she no longer took care of her flowers. They overgrew the paths until the place was a wilderness.

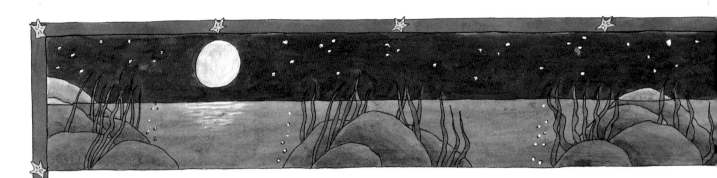

Finally she could bear it no longer. She told her secret to one of her sisters. Immediately all the other sisters heard about it. One of them knew of the prince and knew where his kingdom was.

"Come, little sister!" said the other princesses and, arm in arm, they rose from the water in a long row, right in front of the prince's palace.

Now that she knew where he lived, the little mermaid spent many an evening in a stream beneath the prince's balcony, watching him in the bright moonlight.

Increasingly she grew to like human beings, and more and more she longed to live among them. Their world seemed so much wider than her own, and there was so much about it she wanted to know. Her sisters could not answer all her questions, so she went to her old grandmother.

"If men aren't drowned," the little mermaid asked, "do they live on forever? Don't they die, as we do down here in the sea?"

"Yes," the old lady said, "they, too, must die, and their lifetimes are much shorter than ours. We live to be three hundred years old, but when we perish we turn into foam on the sea. Human beings, on the contrary, are said to have something called a soul, which lives forever after they die and rises through thin air, up to the shining stars."

"Why weren't we given a soul?" the little mermaid asked. "The prince I love has one. In three hundred years, he will be among the stars, and I will be far below, nothing but foam on the sea."

"You must not think about that," said the old lady. "We are much better off than the human folk."

"Can't I do anything at all to win a soul?"

"No," her grandmother answered, "not unless a human loves you so much that you mean more to him than his father and mother. If his every thought and his whole heart bind you together throughout all eternity, then his soul will dwell in your body and you may share in the happiness of humankind. He will give you a soul and yet keep his own."

"But that can never come to pass. Your greatest beauty here in the sea — your fishtail — would be considered ugly on land. To be thought beautiful there, you must have two awkward props they call legs."

The little mermaid sighed and looked unhappily at her tail.

"Oh, let us be happy!" the old lady said. "Let us leap and bound throughout the three hundred years we have to live. Come, we are holding a court ball this evening."

The ball was a glorious affair. Hundreds of huge shells stood in rows. Countless fish swam outside the glass walls of the palace. The mermaids and mermen danced to their own entrancing songs. The little mermaid sang more sweetly than anyone else, and everyone applauded her. For a moment her heart was happy, but her thoughts soon strayed to the prince and to her despair at not having a soul like his. Sadly she stole out of her father's palace and sat in her little garden.

"I know," she said to herself, "I shall visit the sea witch of whom I have always been so afraid. Perhaps she will be able to help me."

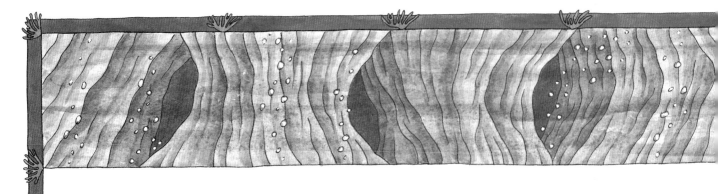

The little mermaid set out from her garden toward the whirlpools that raged in front of the witch's dwelling. No flowers grew there, nor any seaweed. Bare and gray, the sands extended to the whirlpools that pulled everything within their reach down to the bottom of the sea. She had to thread her way between them to reach the witch's waters, and then for a long stretch the only trail lay through a hot, seething mire.

Beyond it, the house lay in the middle of a strange forest, where all the trees and shrubs were polyps, half animal and half plant. They twined around whatever they could lay hold of and never let go.

The little mermaid was terrified and stopped at the edge of the forest. She nearly turned back, but then she remembered the prince and the soul he had, summoned her courage, and darted through the water like a fish among the slimy polyps that stretched out their writhing arms to seize her. She saw that every one of them had something it had caught with its hundreds of tentacles, but the most ghastly sight of all was another little mermaid whom they had caught and strangled.

Finally she reached a large clearing in the forest. In the middle of this clearing was a house built of the bones of shipwrecked men, and outside it sat the sea witch.

"I know exactly what you want," she said. "It is very foolish of you, but you want to get rid of your fishtail and have two props instead so that you can walk about like a human creature, have the young prince fall in love with you, and win him and an immortal soul besides." At this, the witch gave a loud cackling laugh.

"I shall compound you a draught, and before sunrise you must swim to the shore with it, seat yourself on dry land, and drink the draught down. Then your tail will divide and shrink until it becomes what the people on earth call a pair of shapely legs. But it will hurt; it will feel as if a sharp sword is slashing through you.

"Everyone who sees you will say that you are the most graceful human being they have ever seen, for you will keep your gliding movements, and no dancer will be able to tread as lightly as you. But every step you take will feel as if you were treading upon knife blades. Are you willing to suffer all this?"

"Yes," the little mermaid said in a trembling voice.

"Remember!" said the witch. "Once you have taken a human form, you can never be a mermaid again. You can never come back through the waters to your sisters or to your father's palace. And if you do not win the love of the prince, and he marries someone else, your heart will break the very next morning, and you will become foam on the sea."

"I shall take that risk," said the little mermaid, but she turned as pale as death.

"Also, you will have to pay me," said the witch, "and it is no trifling price that I'm asking. You have the sweetest voice of anyone, and you must give this voice to me."

"But if you take my voice," said the little mermaid, "what will be left to me?"

"Your lovely form," the witch told her, "your gliding movements, and your eloquent eyes. With these you can easily enchant a human heart. Now, stick out your tongue, and I shall cut it off. I'll have my price, and you shall have legs."

"Go on, then," said the little mermaid.

The witch hung her caldron over the flames to brew the draught. Then she pricked herself in the chest and let her black blood splash into the caldron. Steam swirled up from it in such ghastly shapes that anyone would have been terrified by them.

"There's your draught," said the witch. And she cut off the little mermaid's tongue. Unable now to sing or talk, she made her way back and rose up through the dark blue sea.

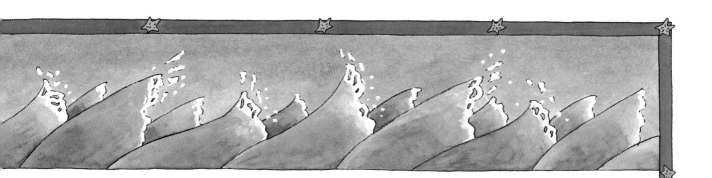

The sun had not yet risen when the little mermaid reached the beach and saw the prince's palace. She swallowed the bitter, fiery draught and felt as if a sword had struck through her body. She swooned away and lay as if dead. When the sun rose over the sea, she awoke and felt a flash of pain, but directly in front of her stood the prince, gazing at her with his coal-black eyes. She saw that her fish-tail was gone and, in its place, was a lovely pair of legs. She was naked, so she covered herself with her long hair.

The prince asked who she was and how she came to be there. She looked at him tenderly but very sadly, for she could not speak. Then he took her hand and led her into his palace. Every footstep felt as if she were walking on sharp knives, just as the witch had foretold, but she endured it. The prince and all who saw her marveled at the grace of her gliding walk.

She was the loveliest person in all the palace, though she could neither sing nor speak. She charmed everyone, especially the prince. She danced time and again, though whenever she touched the floor she felt as if she were treading on sharp-edged steel. The prince said he would keep her with him always.

At night in the prince's palace, while the others slept, the little mermaid would go down the marble steps to cool her burning feet in the cold seawater and remember those who lived beneath the sea. One night her sisters came by, arm in arm, singing sadly. They came to see her every night after that, and once, far, far out to sea, she saw her grandmother, who had not been up to the surface for many years. With her was the sea king, his crown upon his head. They stretched out their hands to her, but they did not venture so near the land as her sisters had.

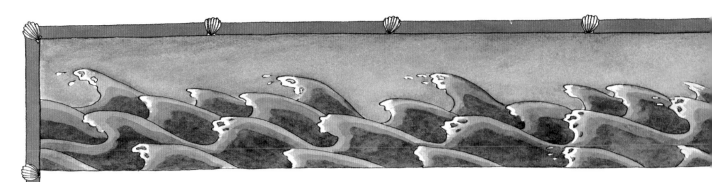

"Don't you love me best of all?" the little mermaid questioned the prince one day with her eyes.

"Yes, you are most dear to me," said the prince, "for you love me more than anyone else does, and you look so much like a girl I once saw but never shall find again. I was on a ship that was wrecked in a storm, and this girl found me beside the sea and saved my life. Though I saw her no more than twice, she is the only person in all the world whom I could love. But you are so much like her that you almost replace the memory of her in my heart."

"Alas, he doesn't know it was I who saved his life," the little mermaid thought.

Now rumors arose that the prince was to wed the beautiful daughter of a neighboring king, and he planned a splendid journey to visit her kingdom. "I am forced to go," he told the little mermaid. "I must visit the princess, for this is my parents' wish. But I can never love her. She does not resemble the lovely maiden who rescued me, as you do, and if I were to choose a bride, I would sooner choose you." And he kissed her and laid his head against her heart in such a way that she came to dream of mortal happiness.

"I trust you aren't afraid of the sea, my silent one," he said as she accompanied him on board the magnificent vessel that was to carry them to the land of the neighboring king. And he told her stories of storms, of ships becalmed, of strange deep-sea fish, and of the wonders that divers had seen. She smiled at such stories, for no one knew about the bottom of the sea as well as she.

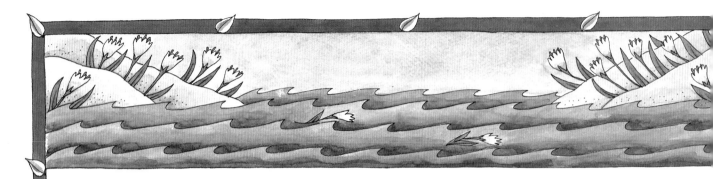

Next morning the ship came into the harbor of the neighboring king's glorious city. All the church bells chimed, and trumpets were sounded from all the high towers. There was a new festivity every day, as one ball followed another, but the princess was still to appear. At last, she arrived.

The little mermaid was curious to see how beautiful this princess was, and she had to grant that she had never seen a more exquisite figure. The princess's skin was clear and fair, and behind the long, dark lashes her deep blue eyes were smiling.

"It was you!" the prince cried. "You are the one who saved me when I lay like a dead man beside the sea." He clasped her in his arms. "Oh, I am happier than a man should be!" he told his little mermaid. "My fondest dream has come true!"

The little mermaid felt her heart beginning to break with sadness, for she knew she had lost her true love, and the morning after his wedding day would see her dead and turned to watery foam.

All the church bells rang and heralds rode through the streets to announce the wedding. The little mermaid, clothed in silk and gold, held the bride's train, but she was deaf to the wedding march and blind to the holy ritual. Her thoughts turned to her last night on earth and to all she had lost in this world.

That same evening, the bride and bridegroom went aboard the prince's ship. Cannons thundered and banners waved.

Brightly colored lanterns were lighted. But the little mermaid could not forget the very first time she rose from the depths of the sea and looked on at such pomp and happiness. She knew this was the last evening she ever would see the prince for whom she had forsaken her home and family, for whom she had sacrificed her lovely voice and suffered such torment. It was the last night that she would breathe the same air as he or look on deep waters or blue sky. Since she had no soul and could not get one, a never-ending night, without thought and without dreams, awaited her. The merrymaking lasted long after midnight, and she laughed and danced despite the thoughts of death she carried in her heart. The prince kissed his beautiful bride, and she caressed his coal-black hair. Hand in hand, they went to rest in the magnificent pavilion.

A hush came over the ship. Only the helmsman remained on deck as the little mermaid leaned her white arms on the bulwarks and looked to the east to see the first red hint of daybreak. Then she saw her sisters rise up among the waves. They were as pale as she, and their lovely long hair had all been cut off.

"We have given our hair to the witch," they said, "so she would send you help and save you from death tonight. She gave us a knife. Here it is. See the sharp blade! Before the sun rises, you must strike it into the prince's heart, and when his warm blood bathes your feet, they will grow together and become a fishtail. Then you will be a mermaid again, able to come back to us and live out your three hundred years before you die and turn into foam on the sea. Make haste! Kill the prince and come back to us. Hurry! See that red glow in the heavens! In a few minutes the sun will rise and you must die." So saying, they gave her the knife and sank beneath the waves.

The little mermaid parted the purple curtains of the tent and saw the beautiful bride asleep with her head on the prince's breast. The mermaid bent down and kissed his forehead. She looked at the sky, fast reddening for the break of day. She looked at the knife and again turned her eyes toward the prince, who in his sleep murmured the name of his bride. The knife blade trembled in the mermaid's hand. But then she flung it far out over the waves. Where it fell, the waves were red, as if bubbles of blood seethed in the water.

Then she looked once more at the prince, hurled herself over the bulwarks into the sea, and felt her body dissolve into foam.

At that moment, the sun rose from beneath the waters. Its beams fell, warm and kindly, upon the chill sea, and the little mermaid did not feel the hand of death. Instead, she gradually rose up out of the foam.

"Who are you, toward whom I rise?" she asked, and her voice suddenly sounded so spiritual that no music on earth could match it.

"Little mermaid," said a voice as wide as the sky, "you have tried with your whole heart to love. Your suffering and your loyalty have raised you up into the realm of spirits, and now you have earned by your good deeds a soul that will never die."

The little mermaid lifted her clear bright eyes toward the sun, and for the first time her eyes were wet with tears.

On board the ship all was astir and lively again. She saw the prince and his fair bride in search of her. Then they gazed sadly into the seething foam, as if they knew she had hurled herself into the waves. Unseen by them, she kissed the bride, smiled at the prince, and rose up to the rose-red clouds that sailed on high.

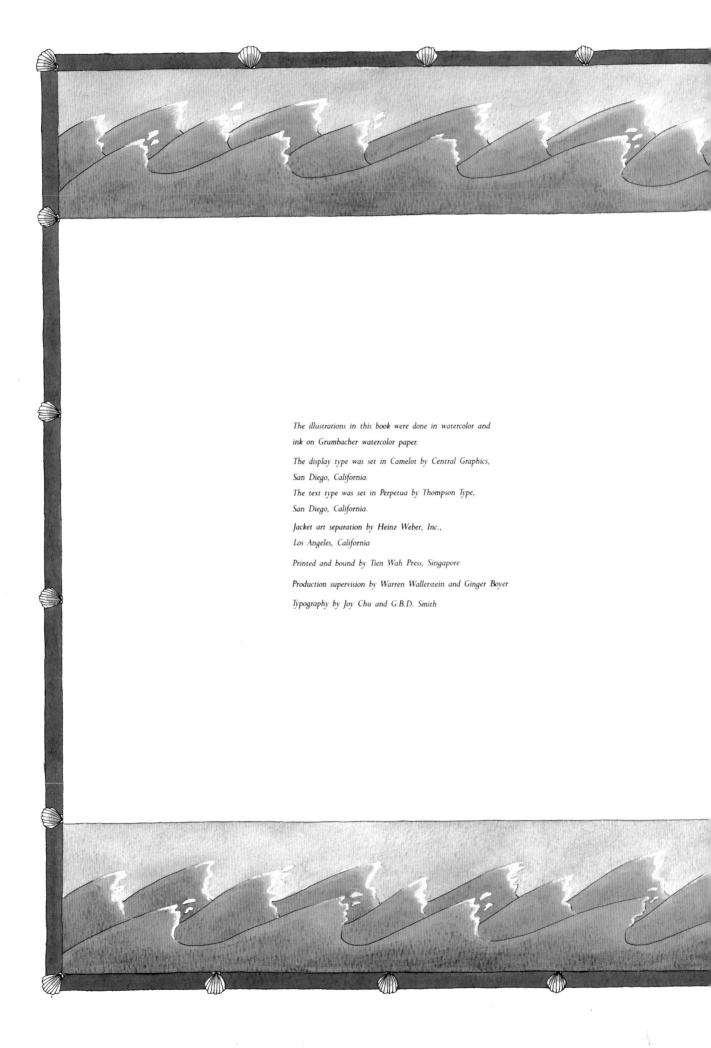

The illustrations in this book were done in watercolor and ink on Grumbacher watercolor paper.

The display type was set in Camelot by Central Graphics, San Diego, California.

The text type was set in Perpetua by Thompson Type, San Diego, California.

Jacket art separation by Heinz Weber, Inc., Los Angeles, California

Printed and bound by Tien Wah Press, Singapore

Production supervision by Warren Wallerstein and Ginger Boyer

Typography by Joy Chu and G.B.D. Smith